Jeannie Ann's Grandma Has Breast Cancer

By Diane Davies

Illustrated by CA Nobens

To families facing breast cancer. May a cure be found.
–DD

To my Auntie Vera, Susan, Jan, and others who've fought so hard.
-CA N

ISBN 13: 978-1-64343-991-4
Library of Congress Catalog Number:
2018961775
Printed in the United States of America
First Printing: 2019
23 22 21 20 19   5 4 3 2 1

Edited by Nancy Crocker
Illustrated and designed by CA Nobens

BEAVER'S POND
PRESS

Beaver's Pond Press, Inc.
7108 Ohms Lane
Edina, MN 55439-2129
(952) 829-8818
www.BeaversPondPress.com

To order, visit www.ItascaBooks.com or call (952) 345-4488. Reseller discounts available.

For more about the author, visit www.DianeDavies.com.

Hi! I'm Jeannie Ann. I have thick, curly hair and freckles on my nose. I live in an ordinary home with my ordinary family. I'm in first grade, and I LOVE school. I love lunch, recess, gym class, math, and science. And I love books, so I think the library is the greatest!

When I get home from school, Mom always gives me a big hug
and a snack. After that, I get to play with my baby brother.

But one day, Mom's hug is extra tight. She forgets my snack, and I see that my baby brother still has his pajamas on. Something is wrong, for sure.

The telephone rings, and after Mom answers it, she starts to cry. I wonder if I've done something to make her sad.

At dinner that night, Mom and Dad don't talk much until after I'm excused from the table. I think I must have done something really bad for them to act that way.

I hang around the kitchen door to see if I can hear what they are whispering about. I hear the word CANCER and get really scared. I know that cancer makes people sick, and sometimes they even die.

I have to know who has cancer. Is it me?
Is it Mom or Dad, or my baby brother?

When Mom tucks me in later, I ask her if I have cancer.
"Oh my goodness—no!" she says. "We were talking about
your grandma. She has breast cancer, and I'm sad for her
because I know she will go through a lot in treatment."

Did you know that the two rounded areas on people's chests are called breasts? I didn't!

"Women can get breast cancer," Mom tells me, "and so can men, sometimes."

(Men have breasts too. They're just smaller.)

She says, "You can't catch breast cancer like a cold or the flu." I'm very glad to hear that!

Mom and I pray together that Grandma's treatment will go well.

I have a lot more questions to ask, but I know Mom and Dad will tell me the answers soon. They're pretty smart that way.

Going to visit Grandma is hard for me. I don't know what to say, so I just give her a big hug and kiss.

She sits with me and explains that our bodies are made up of tiny building blocks called cells. She says we are always making new cells to take over for the old ones.

"But sometimes," she says, "a mistake happens. A healthy new cell doesn't replace the old one. Many, many copies of the odd cell get made instead and begin to pile up. That's called a tumor."

That can be the start of cancer.

Grandma says, "That is what happened in my breast, honey."

Understanding more about cancer helps me feel like an important part of the family and like I'm helping Grandma get better.

I ask her, "Is it scary?"

She nods. "A little bit."

I pat her hand. "I understand. I used to be afraid of the dark."

After a few weeks, Grandma goes to the hospital for an operation
called a mastectomy. Mom tells me this big word means that
the doctor is removing Grandma's breast with the tumor in it.
Her chest is sore there for a long time after,
so we have to give up hugs for a while.
That's tough.

When Grandma is healed from the operation,
she starts taking chemotherapy—chemo, for short.
Chemo is a special medicine that travels through her whole body
and kills any cancer cells that got left behind during her surgery.

Grandma's chemo makes all of her hair fall out. Her head feels soft and smooth, like my baby brother's did when he was born. Mom and I bring her some pretty scarves and hats to wear until it grows back. Grandma says she wants her hair to come back curly so she will look more like me!

The chemo also makes Grandma feel sick, like she needs to throw up. Poor Grandma! But she says, "When I feel sick to my stomach, I just keep telling myself that's the chemo working to kill off the cancer cells. That makes me feel better."

Hearing that makes me feel better too.

We are learning how to read in school, and now I know the word c-a-n-c-e-r when I see it on TV, or in a magazine, or online, or in the newspaper. It's all over the place—even on signs along the highway!

Grandma tells me that if I have questions about her cancer, I should never be afraid to ask her. "If I don't know the answer, I'll help you find it," she says.

So I ask, "Does cancer hurt?"

I know I have asked an important question, because Grandma puts on her thinking face. "Well," she says, "hurt can mean a lot of things. It hurts when you fall off of your bicycle and scrape your knee. Hurt can mean a sore back, or a stubbed toe! The kind of hurt that has to do with your body is called physical pain."

"But hurt can also be emotional pain, meaning it comes from inside you, from your feelings. Emotional pain is like when you feel sad because your best friend moves away, or someone you thought was a friend tells stories about you that aren't true.

"Remember how sad you were when you moved to your new apartment and you had to give Snookles away?"

I remember, all right! Tears water up my eyes.
"Snookles was my dog for my whole life!" I sniffle.

Grandma nods. "Emotional pain hurts in a way that a bandage or a cast can't fix."

I have to know. I make myself ask, "So does cancer hurt?"

Grandma sighs. "That is a really tough question. Some cancer causes physical pain. Most cancer causes emotional pain for the person who has it and also for their family and friends. Cancer can make our feelings hurt, way down deep inside."

I ask, "Does knowing that someone loves you help that kind of hurt, Grandma?"

"Most definitely!" she says with a great big hug.
It feels so good to hug her again!

Well . . . guess what?

All of that happened way back last year! I'm in second grade now, and my grandma is so much better. Her hair's even grown back! It's still gray, but it is really curly, just like mine!

And you know what? Grandma has two breasts again. When I notice lumps under her shirt, I ask, "Grandma, why do you still have two? I thought the doctor removed one."

"He did!" she says. "But I got to decide how I wanted to look after my operation. I could have a flat chest on one side, or have a pretend breast put inside my body during surgery, or wear a pretend breast outside my body, in my underclothes. I decided to wear a pretend breast in my bra."

I'm not glad that Grandma had breast cancer, but I sure am glad that she's happy and healthy again. Once a month, she gets together with some other ladies who had breast cancer too. They are called her support group. They help each other stay well, and they talk about those emotional pains.

I know that some families are not as lucky as mine. Sometimes cancer keeps growing and growing, and even the chemo can't stop it. When that happens, the people can't get better, and they die. Mom and I pray for people who have died from cancer, and their families too.

These days when I come home from school, Mom gives me
a sunny smile and a great big hug. She always remembers
my snack, and I have even more fun playing with my brother
now that he's not a baby anymore. I still have thick, curly hair
and freckles on my nose. I still LOVE school—lunch, recess,
gym class, math, science, and reading!

I still live in an ordinary home with my ordinary family. I know how much
I love them and how much they love me. And even more than ever before,
I know that love is some pretty powerful stuff.

Some suggestions for you and your children when a family member is diagnosed with cancer:

1. **Listen** – Good communication helps everyone in the family cope with whatever changes lie ahead.
2. **Listen** – Talking with your children honestly and helping them express their emotions will help them feel safe and secure.
3. **Listen** – There is no age limit for the need to cry.
4. **Listen** – Sharing information early on will help build trust.
5. **Listen** – Be sure to ask if they have questions. If you don't know the answers, assure them that you will find out.
6. **Listen** – Consider your child's age and keep in mind there is no need to talk beyond what is asked.
7. **Listen** – Let your children know that what they are feeling is normal and okay.
8. **Listen** – Be honest and hopeful.
9. **Listen** – Make sure your children know that nothing they did or said caused the cancer.
10. **Listen** – Keep your children informed throughout the cancer journey.

Resources

CancerCare
800-813-HOPE (4673)

American Cancer Society
800-227-2345

Kids Konnected
800-899-2866

National Cancer Institute
800-422-6237

"Helping Children When a Family Member Has Cancer," CancerCare,
https://www.cancercare.org/publications/22-
helping_children_when_a_family_member_has_cancer

KidsHealth.org

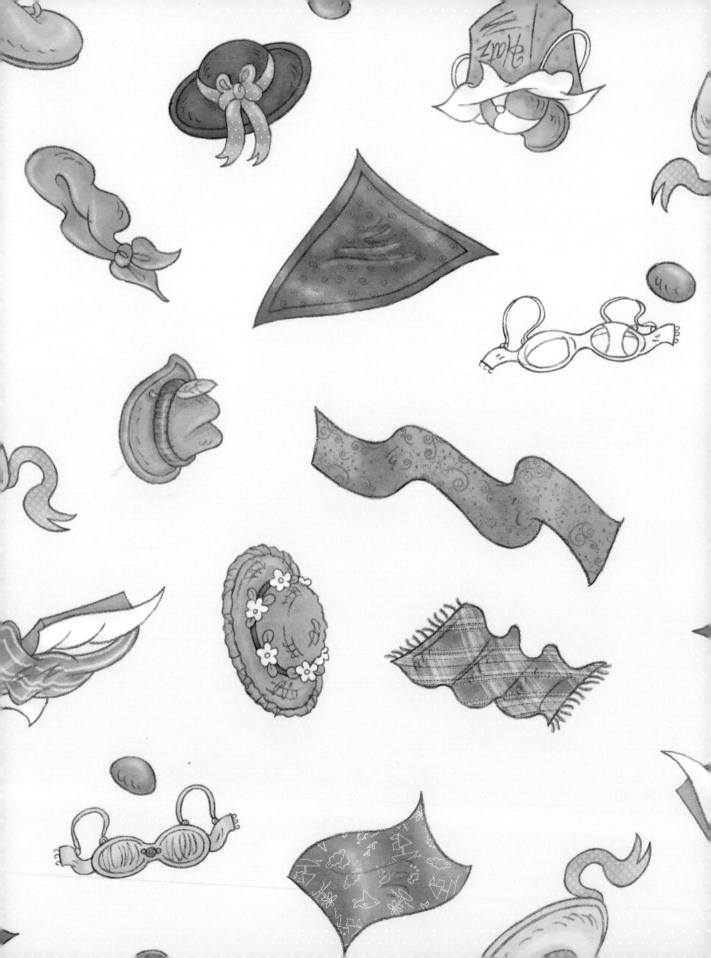